CATSUP HIGH
DETECTIVE AGENCY

MARGARET RYAN

ILLUSTRATED BY
VICKY BARKER

Also by Margaret Ryan:

Roodica the Rude and the Famous Flea Trick
Roodica the Rude and the Chariot Challenge
Roodica the Rude: Who Stole the River?
Roodica the Rude: Party Pooper

CATNIP BOOKS
Published by Catnip Publishing Ltd
320 City Road
London EC1V 2NZ
www.catnippublishing.co.uk

This edition first published 2015

1 3 5 7 9 10 8 6 4 2

Text © Margaret Ryan 2015
Illustration and cover design © Vicky Barker

ISBN 978-1-84647-189-6

Printed and bound by CPI Group (UK) Ltd, Croydon, CR0 4YY

FOR SOPHIE
with love.

PERFECT HARMONY

1. The Catsup High Detective Agency
2. Katya's Beauty Parlour
3. Petrowski's Pet Shop
4. Dogsbody's Cattery
5. Cat's Eyes Optician
6. Cat a Manger
7. Bakery
8. Town Hall
9. Boutique El Cats
10. The Catue of Liberty

CATSUP HIGH DETECTIVE AGENCY:

CASE NUMBERS 46 TO 54

CHAPTER ONE

Malarkey, owner of the Catsup High Detective Agency, was worried. His fur stood up, his tale drooped down and his whiskers quivered like an out of tune violin. He chewed anxiously on the ends of his magic flying scarf.

'I'm really worried,' he said to no one in particular, for his tiny office on Catsup High Street in the little town of Catsup was empty, if you didn't count the family of mice who lived in the hole in the skirting board, or the spider busy making a delicate web curtain at the window. The mice pricked up their ears and stopped in their daily task of devouring the carpet. The spider stopped mid spin and dropped down on a silken thread to listen more closely.

'Why are so many cats in Catsup disappearing?' asked Malarkey.

'That's nine reported missing so far this week already.'

'Seven,' squeaked the mice.

'I think you'll find that the difference between forty-six and fifty-four is eight,' said the spider silkily.

'Smarty pants,' muttered the mice.

'One does one's best,' smiled the spider.

'Well, seven, eight or nine, it's too many,' said Malarkey. 'I can't search for all of them myself and Mayor Mogsworthy says he'll have to employ another detective if I don't get some results soon.

I need some help or I'll lose my job. I'd better advertise for an assistant.'

'Make sure he likes mice,' said the mice.

'And isn't afraid of spiders,' said the spider.

Malarkey dipped his claws in some ink and wrote out a poster. He put it in his office window.

VACANCY FOR
ASSISTANT CAT DETECTIVE

MUST BE HARD WORKING

AND NOT EAT MUCH

SPECIAL POWERS

AN ADVANTAGE

And he sat back and waited. But not for long.

Soon there was a knock on the door.

'Enter,' said Malarkey.

The old door creaked slowly open and a large dog waddled in. The mice scattered in alarm, while the spider curled itself up into a ball and played dead.

'I saw your advert,' said the dog, heaving himself up on to the chair in front of Malarkey's desk. 'I want to apply for the job.'

'It's a job for a cat,' said Malarkey. 'Can't you read? This

is a cat detective agency. The clue is in the word "cat".'

The dog thought for a moment. 'How about if I wear a catsuit, would that help? And I could learn to miaow. How hard can that be? MI . . . UFF MI . . . UFF. Pretty good, huh?'

'Sorry.' Malarkey shook his head.

'Suit yourself,' shrugged the dog and waddled off.

Malarkey settled down to wait some more.

Soon there was another knock and a one-eared white cat with a black eye and several missing teeth wandered in.

'I've come about the job,' he lisped.

'What's your name?' asked Malarkey,

inky claw at the ready to make some notes.

'Champion.'

'Good name. Any special powers?'

'I can tap dance on the white piano keys and I'm good at fighting.'

Malarkey looked at the cat's battered face.

'Looks to me like you're good at losing. Sorry, but I don't think you're quite right for the job.'

'That's all right.' The cat wasn't offended. 'I hear the circus is in town.

Maybe they're looking for a tap-dancing cat.' And he wandered off.

A furry feline wearing a pink diamante collar slid round his door next.

'I'm Felicity Fiona Fortesque-Ffyfe,' she purred. 'But my friends call me Fifi. I've come about the job vacancy. I'd be an excellent cat detective. I can detect right away that even with your big scarf on, you're definitely a cat.'

'Any special powers?' sighed Malarkey.

'Just being beautiful,' smiled Fifi. 'I find I don't need anything else.'

'Well, I do,' said Malarkey. 'Close the door behind you.'

He sighed, leaned back in his chair and put his back paws up on the desk. Then he leaned back some more, fell over and clattered to the ground.

'We've told you about doing that,' tutted the mice. 'Makes us nearly jump right out of our skins, it does. We'll be running around in our bones any day now.'

'It has all to do with your centre of gravity, Malarkey,' said the spider, climbing back up to his web. 'You never learn.'

Malarkey muttered darkly and righted his chair as the door to his office creaked open again. He looked round, but saw nobody. Then a small stripy kitten jumped up on to the chair in front of his desk.

'You're in the wrong place, little kitty,' he said. 'The Kittycat Playgroup is two doors down.'

But the kitten just eyed him solemnly and didn't move.

'I've come about the job vacancy,' he said.

Malarkey laughed. 'I don't think so, little kitty. Come back when you're older and I'll think about it.'

But the kitten still didn't move.

'I don't eat much and I have special powers,' he said.

'Like what?' grinned Malarkey. 'Can you drink all your bedtime milky in one big slurp?'

'Not yet,' admitted the kitten. 'But I could write up your cases for the *Daily Mews* and I could make the ceiling light fall on your head, if you like.'

Malarkey looked up at the light hanging above his head. 'Yeah, yeah,' he said. 'A likely tale.'

'It's no tale,' said the kitten and stretched out a tiny paw.

Sparks of electricity shot out from his claws and burned through the light cable.

The light promptly fell down on Malarkey's head.

'Cool,' said the spider, impressed.

'Awesome!' the mice clapped their claws. 'Do some more! Do some more!'

'No more!' Malarkey rubbed the lump rising between his ears. 'How did you do that?'

'I told you,' said the kitten. 'I have special powers. I'm still discovering new ones.'

'I see.' Malarkey was thoughtful. 'That could certainly be useful. Detecting is a dangerous business. But you're very little. I don't know if you could keep up. What did you say your name was?'

'Sparkie,' said the kitten.

'Okay,' said Malarkey. 'I'll give you a trial, Sparkie, and see how it goes. Now the cases I'm working on concern the disappearance of nine cats.'

'Seven,' said the mice.

'Eight,' sighed the spider.

'Actually I think it might be ten,' said Sparkie. 'I've just seen Champion and Fifi being bundled into the back of a big white van and driven away.'

'I don't suppose you got the registration

number,' asked Malarkey hopefully.

'Of course I did,' said Sparkie. 'I have a photographic memory. It was MR B1G.'

CHAPTER TWO

'Mr Big?' Malarkey rubbed his chin. 'Sounds impressive.'

'Sounds scary,' muttered the mice.

'Sounds like you need to get to work, Malarkey,' said the spider. 'I'll mind the store.'

'Okay.' Malarkey got down to business. 'Now listen carefully, Sparkie. There are three rules a good detective must follow. Rule number one: Look for clues.'

'Look for clues. Got it,' said Sparkie.

'Rule number two: Gather information.'

'Gather information. Got it,' said Sparkie.

'Rule number three . . . er . . . rule number three is . . . now, what was rule number three?'

'Catch the bad guys?' suggested Sparkie.

'You got it. Now let's go. Hold on to my scarf and we'll fly over to Katya's Beauty Parlour. Katya may have heard something about the missing cats.'

Sparkie held on tightly while Malarkey hurtled down Catsup High Street. Gathering speed, he just managed to take off before they ploughed into a cluster of wheelie bins. They headed up and over the rooftops. Sparkie kept his head down when several large chimney pots loomed close, then eventually Malarkey landed with

a thud just outside Katya's Beauty Parlour.
But the place was looking anything but
beautiful.

The outside of the shop was covered
in graffiti.

'**ALL CATS ARE BATS**,' read Sparkie.
'**MICE RULE THE WORLD**.'

Inside, Katya was in tears.

'Oh, Malarkey,' she sobbed. 'Just look at the mess. It'll take me ages to clean it off. Business was bad enough before with all the cats disappearing, but this may just close me down. Who could have done it?'

'I don't know.' Malarkey was grim. 'But Sparkie and I intend to find out.' He roamed round the shop lifting up combs, brushes and bottles of shampoo, looking for clues. 'Unfortunately they don't seem to have left us any clues,' he sighed.

'What about the big handprint in red paint on the shop window?' said Sparkie. 'Is that not a clue?'

'What? Oh yes. I saw that, of course. I was just testing to see if you had. Go and examine it, then we'll go to Mr Petrowski's Pet Shop and see if there are any more clues there.'

Mr Petrowski was mending the broken lock on his front door when they thumped down on his doorstep.

'Aha!' cried Malarkey. 'I detect that someone has tried to break in here.'

'**NOT TRIED! SUCCEEDED!**' yelled Mr Petrowski. 'I came in this morning to find the front door hanging open and all my stock damaged.'

Malarkey and Sparkie went inside the shop to have a look. It wasn't good. Cages had been knocked over and rabbits and guinea pigs were hopping about among the sawdust and cat litter. Dried cat food lay scattered across the floor.

'What a mess,' said Malarkey, picking up a toy mouse and giving it a squeak. 'I don't know how Mr Petrowski will carry on after this. He was already losing business because of the missing cats.'

'Well, what are you going to do about it, Malarkey?' demanded Mr Petrowski, coming inside to look for a bigger screwdriver. 'You're the town detective.'

'I know.' Malarkey chewed on a bit of cat food. 'And I assure you, Sparkie and I are on the case. But the vandals don't seem to have left us any clues.'

'What about those big footprints in the

sawdust?' said Sparkie. 'They're far too big
to belong to Mr Petrowski. Are they not a
clue?'

'What? Oh yes. I saw them, of course.
I was just testing to see if you had. Go
and examine them, then we'll go to Mrs
Dogsbody's Cattery and see if there are
any more clues there.'

Mrs Dogsbody was sitting among the empty cages in her cattery when Malarkey and Sparkie arrived. Malarkey was nursing a sore back paw.

'I don't think you should have attempted that one paw landing on to the scratching post,' gasped Sparkie. 'My stripes are still quivering!'

'I'll get it right one of these days,' muttered Malarkey. 'There must be a way to do it. Now, Mrs Dogsbody,' he went on. 'How are all your cats today?'

Mrs Dogsbody looked at him in amazement. 'What cats? Can't you see that they've gone?' She pointed to the empty cages. 'Every last furry feline. Stolen from their little beds in the night, they were.

I heard nothing. Not a miaow. Not a wail. Nothing. What am I going to do? No one will ever trust me with their cats again. I will have to close down.'

'Not if we know anything about it,' said Malarkey. 'Sparkie and I are here to help. We're here to look for clues. Have you seen any, Sparkie?' he asked hopefully.

'What kind of vehicle do you drive, Mrs Dogsbody,' asked Sparkie.

'I have a big three-wheeler bike with a trailer attached,' she said.

'Then those large tyre tracks on the driveway aren't yours?'

Mrs Dogsbody looked. 'Certainly not,' she said. 'And they weren't there yesterday.'

'I wondered if you would spot that clue, Sparkie,' said Malarkey. 'You're doing very well. Now go and examine the tyre tracks, then we'll be off.'

When they got back to the Catsup High Detective Agency, Malarkey sat at his big desk to have a think. He put his back paws up on the desk and said, 'Let's mull over what we've got so far. Sparkie, you begin the mulling.'

The mice came out of their hole in the skirting board and sat on their haunches to have a listen. The spider dropped down on a silken thread.

'Well,' said Sparkie, 'we know that Katya's Beauty Parlour was vandalised by someone with a very big hand.' He dipped his tiny claws in the ink and drew the size of it on some paper.

'Big hand,' agreed the mice. 'HUGE.'

'Extra large in the glove department,' nodded the spider.

'And we know Mr Petrowski's Pet Shop was broken into by someone with very big feet.' He dipped his tiny claws into the ink and drew the size of them.

'Big feet,' agreed the mice. 'Both of them.'

'Enormous in the shoe department,' nodded the spider.

'And we know that whoever stole Mrs Dogsbody's cats was driving something with very big tyres.' He dipped his tiny claws into the ink and drew the size and the pattern of the tyres.

'Could be a bus,' said the mice.

'No,' said the spider. 'More likely to be a large windowless van with room in the back for the cats.'

'Like the van I saw driving off,' said Sparkie. 'The van with the registration number MR B1G.'

CHAPTER THREE

'Right, Sparkie,' said Malarkey. 'Time to look further afield for the missing cats. We need to widen our search. We need to take to the skies. We need to zoom over the wide blue yonder. We need to go on a dangerous mission of mercy to rescue the missing moggies.'

'Stop talking and just get on with it, Malarkey,' muttered the mice. 'Our fur will have turned white and our whiskers fallen off by the time you're through.' And they went back to nibbling the carpet.

'Better fasten your seat belt, Sparkie,'

advised the spider. 'Malarkey failed arm-flapping at flight school. He should still have L-plates stuck to his stern.' And he went back to some serious web-spinning.

Malarkey ignored them. 'Hold on tight for a vertical takeoff, Sparkie,' he said, and took a deep breath.

'Shouldn't we go outside first?' suggested Sparkie. 'You've already got a bump on your head.'

Outside, Sparkie held on tightly to Malarkey's long scarf as he attempted a vertical takeoff. But, after a few moments of hopping up and down and getting nowhere, Malarkey gave in and broke into a run. Eventually they took off, narrowly missing a pushchair, a post box and a petrified pensioner.

They flew all round the little town of Catsup.

'Look out for anything suspicious,' Malarkey ordered.

'And you look out for kitten-eating crows,' muttered Sparkie, coming nose to beak with an evil-looking specimen.

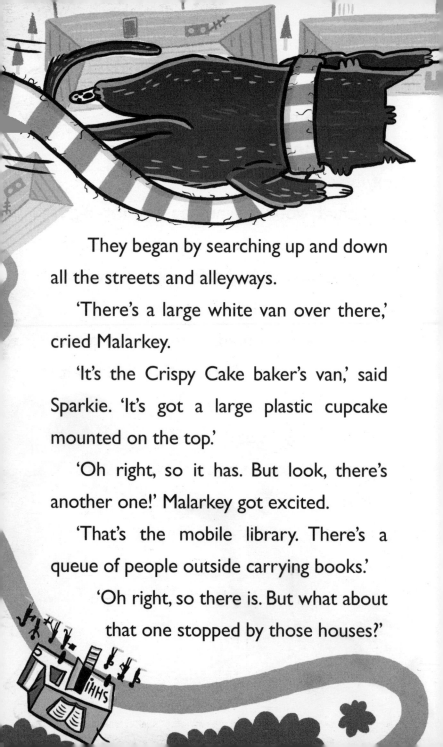

They began by searching up and down all the streets and alleyways.

'There's a large white van over there,' cried Malarkey.

'It's the Crispy Cake baker's van,' said Sparkie. 'It's got a large plastic cupcake mounted on the top.'

'Oh right, so it has. But look, there's another one!' Malarkey got excited.

'That's the mobile library. There's a queue of people outside carrying books.'

'Oh right, so there is. But what about that one stopped by those houses?'

'Ice-cream van,' sighed Sparkie. 'I think the musical chimes may be a clue.'

'I think you're right, Sparkie. Mr Big's been very clever. It's going to be much harder than I thought to spot his white van.'

'Perhaps he wouldn't leave it in plain sight,' said Sparkie. 'Perhaps he's hidden it in a shed or an outhouse.'

'I was just going to say that,' said Malarkey. 'Time to search all the gardens.'

It sounded like a good idea, but proved to be tricky for three reasons.

ONE: Some of the gardens were so overgrown it was like landing in a jungle and Sparkie had to sit on Malarkey's head to direct him to the sheds.

'Go left, Malarkey. Go left . . . No, try your other left . . .'

TWO: Some of the gardens preferred to grow junk instead of grass.

'Imagine collecting shopping trolleys,' said Malarkey. 'I wonder what they use them for and I wonder what they keep in the sheds?'

'More shopping trolleys,' said Sparkie, standing on Malarkey's shoulders and peering in through the dusty windows.

THREE: Some of the gardens had large dogs. Large dogs who didn't care much for cats.

'I know what we'll do,' said Malarkey,

when they had been chased off several times. 'I'll hover above the sheds and lower you down on the end of my scarf. That way you can look in the windows.'

'Okay,' gulped Sparkie, and hoped that Malarkey's hoverings were better than his takeoffs and landings.

But though they looked everywhere there was still no sign of Mr Big's van, and still no sign of the missing cats.

'I detect that there is nothing to be found here,' said Malarkey. 'We'll have to extend our search to the outskirts of town.'

Sparkie agreed and they headed off. But when they had flown round the same large oak tree three times, Sparkie got a bit worried.

'Are you lost, Malarkey?' he asked.

'Of course not. I'm just not sure where I am, that's all. There are no signposts up here, you know.'

'Maybe you should get CATNAV,' suggested Sparkie, and ducked low to avoid a curious seagull.

They continued in ever-widening circles till, after a while, Sparkie spotted an old warehouse.

'Look down there, Malarkey. That looks like it's been newly painted. And in the same colours as the graffiti on Katya's Beauty Parlour.'

'Well spotted, young Sparkie,' said Malarkey, and immediately went into a nosedive to check it out. Sparkie held on to the scarf, and the contents of his tummy, till they levelled out beside the warehouse and cruised round the outside.

'It's all locked up and the windows are boarded over,' said Malarkey. 'It's not what we're looking for. Probably some new supermarket that's about to open up.'

'But it looks nearly ready, so why board up the windows?' said Sparkie. 'And surely there would be signs up advertising the opening date. I think we need to investigate further. Perhaps you should go round the back and see if you can find a way in.'

Malarkey flew round to the back of the warehouse and Sparkie spotted a tiny unboarded window up near the roof.

'If you hover near that window,' he said,

'I could use my special powers to cut our way in.'

Malarkey hovered while Sparkie sat on his shoulders and aimed his little paw at the window's wooden surround. Sparks flew from his claws and burned through the window frame.

'Well done,' said Malarkey, and aimed an unexpected kick at it.

Sparkie tumbled down from his shoulders and only missed plunging to the ground by grabbing the end of Malarkey's scarf.

'Careful you don't fall,' said Malarkey. 'Don't want you losing one of your nine lives.'

Sparkie took a deep breath, climbed back up the scarf on to Malarkey's shoulders and in through the opening. Malarkey followed.

At least he tried to but his scarf got caught on a rusty nail and nearly strangled him.

'He's got me,' he croaked. 'Mr Big has got me. It's all over. Save yourself, little Sparkie. Save yourself! Tell the mice and the spider I love them.'

Sparkie sighed and released him.

'Mr Big could never have got in through that window,' he said.

'Of course not,' gasped Malarkey, aiming for a laugh. 'I knew that. I was only joking.'

The two of them made their way inside. By the light coming from the window opening they could see large packing cases stacked up around the walls.

'See, told you it was a supermarket,' said Malarkey.

But Sparkie wasn't convinced. 'I'd like to know what's in those packing cases,' he said.

'Next time, we'll bring a torch,' said Malarkey. 'All good detectives in the movies carry a torch.'

'No need,' said Sparkie. 'I'll just use one of my special powers.' And he blinked three times and the gleam from his green eyes grew laser-bright till they could clearly make out the writing on the packing cases. Some said:

PAINT: VARIOUS
COLOURS
DELIVER TO MR BIG

Others said:

CAT FOOD:
VARIOUS FLAVOURS
DELIVER TO MR BIG

Yet more said:

CAT TOYS, CAT LITTER,
CAT SHAMPOO, CAT BEDS,
CAT TREATS
DELIVER TO MR BIG

'I fancy the cat treats,' said Malarkey, licking his lips.

'Never mind that,' said Sparkie. 'Look over there.' And he turned his laser-beam eyes on to several large banners that were hung on the walls.

They said:

'Looks like we're in the right place after all,' said Sparkie. 'I bet that's why they're trying to put the other shops out of business.'

Suddenly they heard a noise coming from downstairs.

'What was that?' whispered Malarkey.

'I don't know,' said Sparkie. 'But we don't want to give away our whereabouts.' And he immediately blinked three times

53

and switched off his megawatt eyes. Malarkey gulped. 'Er . . . I don't want to worry you because you're just a little kitten and it's your first day on the job, but you're not used to dangerous detective work like I am. It could be Mr Big and his gang down there. I think we should just go back outside and hide somewhere and watch what happens. Wait till they go away, and then decide what to do. I think that's best, don't you? I promise I won't think you're a scaredy-cat for not going downstairs.'

But there was no reply. Sparkie had already trotted off to investigate.

CHAPTER FOUR

'Sparkie! Sparkie, where are you?' hissed Malarkey. 'Come back. Don't go without me.'

'I'm at the top of the stairs,' whispered Sparkie. 'Come quietly.'

Malarkey felt his way towards the stairs till he touched a furry head and two furry ears. 'I've found one of them, Sparkie.' Malarkey was gleeful. 'I've found one of the missing cats.' And he picked it up.

'You found *me*, Malarkey,' sighed Sparkie. 'Those are my ears you've got. Now put me down and listen ...'

'What for?' Malarkey strained forward, tripped on his long scarf, and tumbled down head over heels, bumping off every stair as he went.

'**OWLLL**,' he cried. '**OWLLL**.'

'**OWLLL, OWLLL**,' the cry was taken up by several other cats.

'Well done, Malarkey,' said Sparkie. 'I think you actually *have* found the cats this time.'

Malarkey stood up and rubbed his rear. 'No problem for an ace detective, but where are they? It's so dark in here I can hardly see a thing.'

He had no sooner spoken when the big double doors of the warehouse were thrown open and light flooded in.

Three very large and one very small man stood in the doorway, silhouetted against the light.

'It's those meddling cat detectives,' snarled the small man. 'They've been making a nuisance of themselves asking questions about me. Poking their noses in. Interfering felines that they are! Get them!'

'Certainly, Mr Big,' grinned the three large men.

Sparkie held on to Malarkey's scarf as he tried to run and take off, but there were too many packing cases in the way, and before they had a chance to escape, the men had grabbed them. They grasped them tightly.

Mr Big smiled evilly. 'Put them in the large hamper with the rest of their furry friends.'

Malarkey struggled as best he could. Sparkie struggled as best he could. But it was no use. The men were too strong for them. A few moments later they found themselves bundled into the hamper beside all the other missing cats.

'Ow, get off,' yelled the cats, as Malarkey and Sparkie landed on top of them. 'There's little enough room as it is!'

'What kept you, Malarkey?' lisped Champion, as the hamper lid crashed down and was fastened shut. 'Call yourself a detective. We thought you'd never get here. Though you're not much good now are you. When they picked me up outside your office I fought them off gum and claw, but they were too strong for me. Did you see the size of their hands and feet?'

'And I told the ruffians to unhand me at once,' said Fifi. 'But they just laughed and pulled my topknot. I dread to think what a state it's in now.'

'We're all in a state,' muttered the other cats.

'I'm starving,' said one.

'I'm thirsty,' said another.

'And I need a wee,' said a third.

'Okay, okay,' said Malarkey. 'Now just all quieten down and let me think about what we should do. Any ideas, Sparkie?'

Sparkie was thoughtful. 'Before we were thrown in here, I thought I caught a glimpse of some hammocks. Are Mr Big and his gang sleeping here?'

'Oh yes,' said Fifi. 'Apparently they snore all night long.

If we don't get out of here, I won't get a wink of beauty sleep.'

'Yeah, we tried to get our own back by howling all night, but they just threw a bucket of cold water over us,' muttered some of the other cats.

'Okay,' said Sparkie. 'In that case, I do have a plan. I can cut us out of here using my special powers, but we need to wait till they've all gone to sleep, then it's time for Operation Cat Flap ...'

The cats listened carefully to Sparkie's plan then settled down to wait.

CHAPTER FIVE

Sparkie sat in a corner of the hamper with his ear to one of the small spaces in the wickerwork.

'What are you listening for?' asked Malarkey. 'I can't hear a thing.'

'I've just discovered another special power,' whispered Sparkie. 'I seem to have developed extra-acute hearing. I can hear Mr Big and his gang talking at the other side of the warehouse. I can hear what they're planning.'

'That will let us know what they're up to,' said Malarkey. 'Good.'

'No, it's not. First thing in the morning they're going to put this hamper into their van and drive to the coast. Then they plan to push us and the hamper out to sea.'

'Oh dear, I've never fancied a cruise,' said Malarkey. 'I get seasick just looking into my water dish.'

'I think it's more serious than that,' said Sparkie. 'This cruise would be to the bottom of the ocean. Not somewhere we'd want to visit, so I'll set Operation Cat Flap in motion just as soon as I can count four sets of snores.'

He carried on listening but he didn't have long to wait. Soon ...

SNORE SNUFFLE SNUFFLE.
SNORK SNIFFLE SNIFFLE.

WHISTLE OOO OOOOO. WHEEEEEEEE UUURKKK.

'Time to go,' whispered Sparkie. He blinked three times and switched on his laser-beam eyes then, stretching out his tiny paw, he used his special powers to cut a cat-flap sized hole in the back of the hamper. The other cats cheered silently then slipped through one by one.

'That's better,' lisped Champion, yawning and stretching. 'My paws have got pins and needles in them and my bum's gone to sleep.'

'I must look a fright,' said Fifi. 'Is there

a mirror in this awful place? I can't see very well in this laser light. Katya's Beauty Parlour has got lots of lights and lots and lots of lovely mirrors.'

'Never mind that now,' said Sparkie. 'Keep very quiet and follow me.'

'Yes. Follow us,' said Malarkey. 'And see what real detectives do.' And he walked off in the wrong direction.

The cats followed Sparkie and watched as he cut open all the packing cases. Then he opened up all the tins of cat food.

'Yummy,' said the cats, and ate their fill.

'Now,' whispered Sparkie, 'I want you

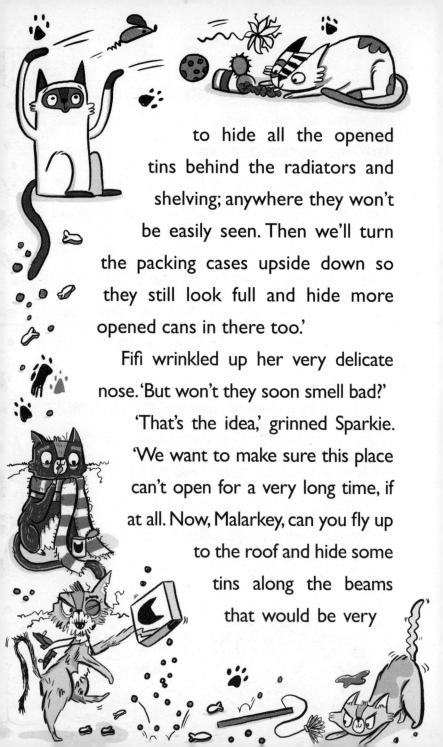

to hide all the opened tins behind the radiators and shelving; anywhere they won't be easily seen. Then we'll turn the packing cases upside down so they still look full and hide more opened cans in there too.'

Fifi wrinkled up her very delicate nose. 'But won't they soon smell bad?'

'That's the idea,' grinned Sparkie. 'We want to make sure this place can't open for a very long time, if at all. Now, Malarkey, can you fly up to the roof and hide some tins along the beams that would be very

hard for anyone to reach.'

'That's no problem for a flying cat detective,' boasted Malarkey, who grabbed some tins and just managed to take off by running along the top of a line of packing cases and launching himself towards the roof.

After that they quietly scattered cat litter, cat toys, cat beds and dried cat food all over the warehouse, even tiptoeing over towards the sleeping gang members and dropping cat food into their big boots.

Finally, Sparkie opened the tins of paint and the cats had a great time dipping their paws in

and leaving paw prints everywhere.

'I haven't done this since I was at Kittycat Playgroup,' grinned Champion. 'Can I jump up leave paw prints all over Mr Big and his gang?'

'In a minute,' grinned Sparkie. 'We have to tie them up in their hammocks first. We'll use their big banners to do that.'

Malarkey and Sparkie took down the banners from the walls and the cats carried them over to the sleeping men. Working in teams of three they quickly wound the cloth banners round and round the unsuspecting men and tied them up tightly with the hanging ropes.

The gang muttered, stirred in their sleep and tried to turn over, but they couldn't.

'Hey,' they yelled, suddenly wakening up.

'What's happening? We can't move. Untie us at once. Let us out of here!'

'No chance,' lisped Champion. 'Let's party, guys.'

And the cats jumped on the hammocks and set to work. Fifi jumped on to the head of the gang member who had catnapped her. 'That's for ruining my topknot,' she said, stamping different-coloured paw prints all over his face.

'Ow, get off!' he spluttered. But she didn't.

Soon the faces and the feet of the men were covered in multi-coloured paw prints.

'That was fun,' gasped Champion, out of breath from tap dancing on the chest of the biggest gang member. 'What else can we do to teach them a lesson?'

'We need to phone the police to come and arrest them,' said Malarkey. 'I'll use one of the gang's mobiles. You lot get home as quickly as you can. Your owners will be waiting.'

'There is just one more thing we *could* do,' grinned Sparkie, while Malarkey was on the phone. 'Before we lock Mr Big and his gang in, we could do this . . .' And he stretched out a tiny paw. Sparks of electricity shot from his claws and all the overhead sprinklers came on.

'Oi, turn those off. We're getting

soaked,' cried the gang.

'No way,' grinned the cats. 'That's payback for the bucket of cold water you threw over us.'

And with a final look at the gang struggling in their hammocks, Malarkey, Sparkie and the cats scampered off, locking the warehouse door behind them.

CHAPTER SIX

Back at the Catsup High Detective Agency the mice and the spider were woken up by Malarkey, as he came skidding to a halt outside the front door and crashed into it head first.

'Who left that door there?' he muttered, and entered the office.

Sparkie slid down Malarkey's long scarf on to the floor and tried to stop shaking.

'There'd better be a good reason for wakening us up at this hour, Malarkey,' said the mice. 'We were having a lovely dream about strawberries and cream.'

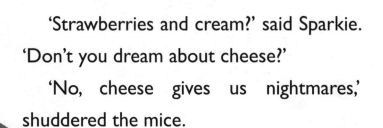

'Strawberries and cream?' said Sparkie.
'Don't you dream about cheese?'

'No, cheese gives us nightmares,'
shuddered the mice.

'Whereas you look like the cat who's got the cream, Malarkey,' said the spider. 'Does this mean you've actually solved cases forty-six to fifty-four?'

'It certainly does,' Malarkey preened. 'They don't call me an ace detective for nothing.'

'They don't call you that at all,' said the spider.

Malarkey ignored him. 'Settle down and pay attention and I'll tell you all about it.'

'Can't it wait till the morning?' yawned the mice. 'We've got a dream to finish. We need to know who got the last strawberry.'

'Late morning would be better for me,' said the spider. 'I've had a tiring day on the web.'

'No, I need to tell you now while I can remember all the details,' said Malarkey. 'I don't want to miss anything out.'

'We were afraid of that,' sighed the mice.

'Extremely afraid,' sighed the spider. Malarkey sat down and put his back paws up on the desk. 'Once upon a time,' he said, 'in a little town called Catsup, there lived a very famous detective called Malarkey . . .'

'ZZZZZ,' said the mice.

'ZZZZ,' said the spider.

By next morning news of the capture of the gang was on Radio Catsup. 'But,' said the newsreader, 'unfortunately it seems that the gang leader got away. He somehow managed to wriggle free from his bonds and escape through a small opening up near the warehouse roof. Police think he may have shinned down the drainpipe and headed for the nearby woods. They are on the lookout for a very small man called Mr Big. People are asked not to approach him as he may be dangerous.'

'Oh no,' said Malarkey. 'After all my hard work, Mr Big is still on the loose!'

'But it was excellent work nonetheless, Malarkey,' Mayor Mogsworthy told him when he called into the Catsup High

Detective Agency next day. 'The cat owners have been on the phone to tell me how delighted they are that all their pets have returned safely. Katya, Mr Petrowski and Mrs Dogsbody have decided they can open up for business again too. And I've decided that you can keep your job as town detective, for the moment at any rate. But tell me, who is this cute little fellow? I haven't seen him before.'

'This is Sparkie,' said Malarkey 'He's very young, just a kitten really. He's here with me on . . . work experience. Just to see how the job is done. Just to see a real detective at work.'

Sparkie licked his little paws but said nothing.

'Good. Good,' said Mayor Mogsworthy. 'Well, keep up the good work. Hopefully that's the last we'll hear of Mr Big.'

'Hopefully,' muttered Sparkie, who wasn't quite so sure.

Some days later it was business as usual at the Catsup High Detective Agency. The mice were busy devouring the carpet, the spider was busy making a delicate web curtain at the window, and Sparkie was busy writing up the Case of the Missing Cats for the *Daily Mews*. Malarkey was busy sitting down in his chair. He leaned back, and put his back paws up on the desk.

'Did I ever tell you about case numbers forty-six to fifty-four? The Case of the Missing Cats?'

'Several times,' muttered the mice.

'Ad nauseam,' said the spider.

'Add what?' asked the mice.

'Till we're sick of hearing about it,' sighed the spider.

But Malarkey wasn't listening.

'I don't want to bore you with the finer details but basically my keen eye picked up some vital clues from the shops in town, then after an extensive search of town premises and gardens . . . at great personal risk, I spotted a warehouse on the outskirts of town that been recently painted – the warehouse that is. Following that, at even greater personal risk, I broke in. That's when Mr Big and the gang grabbed me. I fought them off as best I could but there were four of them and I was overpowered and thrown into a hamper with the rest of the cats. Fortunately I came up with a plan and managed to escape, tie up Mr Big and the gang, and rescue the cats.'

'And what about Sparkie?' asked the mice.

'He was there too,' admitted Malarkey. 'He was quite helpful really.'

'So you'll definitely be hiring him,' said the spider. 'If he was *quite* helpful.'

'Well, I don't know yet. I'll have to see. I'll have to think about it. I'll—'

'Oh, I forgot to tell you,' said the spider. 'Just before you appeared this morning, another case came in. It seems there's been a number of serious crimes committed in Perfect Harmony.'

'Perfect Harmony?' frowned Malarkey. 'Isn't that the posh village where the mayor lives?'

'It is,' said the spider. 'And the mayor's

not happy. He wants you to go and see him in his office. He wants you to investigate the case right away.'

Malarkey gulped and took his feet off the desk. 'Come on, Sparkie,' he said. 'We need to go. Oh, and by the way, you're hired …'

MEET THE GANG!

MALARKEY:

Likes: Cat treats, cat toys and comfortable cat beds.

Dislikes: Working too hard. Getting up early. Uncomfortable cat beds.

Favourite joke: What do mice do in the daytime? MOUSEWORK!

SPARKIE:

Likes: Looking for clues, solving difficult cases and his cuddly bedtime blanket.

Dislikes: Hailstones bouncing on his head and scary snowmen with carrot noses.

Best magical power: Electric paws!

SPIDER:

Likes: Reading and being on the web.

Dislikes:
Window cleaners. (Have they any idea how long it takes to spin a web!)

Favourite web site:
Malarkey's office window.
www.spider@malarkey's.com

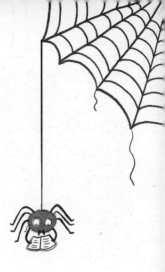

THE MICE:

Like: Nibbling. Nibbling. Nibbling. Dreaming about nibbling.

Dislike: Not nibbling.

Favourite snack:
Chocolate cats.
Good for nibbling.

FIFI:
Likes: Mirrors.
(Except for those in the
Hall of Mirrors at the
fair. They should
be banned!!!)
Dislikes: Anywhere
without a beauty parlour.
Beauty tip: Kitten Pink
is the in colour for nails.

MR BIG:
Likes: BEING BAD!
Dislikes: Being good.
It's rubbish!
Favourite hobby:
Knitting stripy socks.
(His granny taught him.)

3

MARGARET RYAN:

Likes: Writing stories.

Dislikes: Getting stuck at the hard bits.

Favourite joke: THE TRAIN NOW STANDING AT PLATFORMS THREE, FOUR AND FIVE HAS COME IN SIDEWAYS.

VICKY BARKER:

Likes: Drawing pictures.

Dislikes: Spiders - unless they are the monocle wearing kind

Favourite joke: Did you hear about the cat that swallowed a ball of wool? She had mittens!

COMING IN 2016...

CATSUP HIGH DETECTIVE AGENCY:

THE REVENGE OF MR BIG

'I've never visited Perfect Harmony,' said Sparkie. 'Is it a nice place?'

'Very posh,' said the mice, coming out of their hole in the skirting board to eat a bit more of the office carpet. 'We have distant cousins who live there. They dine on proper Persian carpets, not like this threadbare old rag we have to put up with. AND they told us that the mousetraps in Perfect Harmony have Belgian chocolate in them.'

'Did someone mention chocolate?' The office spider stopped mid-spin and dropped down on a silken thread from his web curtain at the window. 'I just love chocolate. Smooth, velvety dark chocolate with just a hint of mandarin is my favourite, though I can be tempted to a coffee cream ...'

'Never mind all this talk about food,' said Malarkey. 'If this case isn't solved quickly Mayor Mogsworthy says Sparkie and I will be out of a job. Then he'll hire another detective who'll probably come in here, board up the mouse hole and clean the window. Then where will you be?'

The mice shuddered and sat back on their haunches. 'Tell us all about it, Malarkey. We're all ears.'

'And legs,' said the spider.

IF YOU ENJOYED CATSUP HIGH DETECTIVE AGENCY, YOU'LL PROBABLY LOVE...

 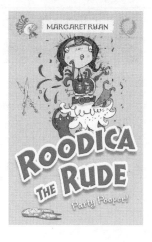

Roodica the Rude by Margaret Ryan, illustrated by Sarah Horne:

Roodica the Rude and the Famous Flea Trick
Roodica the Rude and the Chariot Challenge
Roodica the Rude: Who Stole the River?
Roodica the Rude: Party Pooper

AND...

The *Fabulous Four Fish Fingers* series by
Jason Beresford, illustrated by Vicky Barker:

The Fabulous Four Fish Fingers
Frozen Fish Fingers